Little Sparkles

Party at the Zoo

Collect all the

LITTLE SPARKLES

1. Party in the Garden
2. Party at the Zoo
3. Party at the Pool
4. Party on the Pirate Ship
5. Party in the castle

Little Sparkles

Party at the Zoo

Emily Moon

SCHOLASTIC

First published in the UK in 2012 by Scholastic Children's Books
An imprint of Scholastic Ltd
Euston House, 24 Eversholt Street
London, NW1 1DB, UK
Registered office: Westfield Road, Southam, Warwickshire, CV47 0RA
SCHOLASTIC and associated logos are trademarks and/or
registered trademarks of Scholastic Inc.
Series created by Working Partners Ltd.

Text copyright © Working Partners Ltd., 2012
Illustrations copyright © Dynamo, 2012

ISBN 978 1407 12457 5

Printed and bound by CPI Group (UK) Ltd., Croydon, CR0 4YY
Papers used by Scholastic Children's Books
are made from wood grown in sustainable forests.

1 3 5 7 9 10 8 6 4 2

www.scholastic.co.uk/zone

With special thanks to Dawn McNiff

For Mabel, with love x

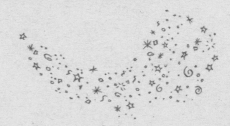

Dear Holly + Rose,

It's my birthday on Saturday.

Please come to the petting zoo at 11 o'clock for a special picnic.

We'll be face-painting and making balloon animals too.

Love,
Billy

1

Who's at the Zoo?

"Wowee," said Rose. She was standing underneath a wooden archway that led into the petting zoo. Bright sunshine danced over the pens and wooden huts. Lush, shady trees waved their branches in the gentle wind, and the pathways were edged with bushes heavy with flowers. Cheeps, baas, oinks and quacks seemed to come from every direction.

Rose's twin sister, Holly, came to stand beside her. "Billy's party is going to be such fun," she said, her eyes shining. "I can't believe that we're going to have the entire petting zoo to ourselves!"

Holly linked her arm through her twin's and spun her round so fast that their sun hats nearly fell off. Their matching polka-dot dresses billowed out and their toffee-coloured plaits swung behind them. They looked exactly the same except for their watches – Holly's was green and Rose's was pink.

BAAA-AAA!

A bleating noise was coming from one of the pens, and Holly and Rose ran to have a look. A mother goat and her three kids were munching on the grass. One of the kids looked up at the girls and skipped towards them. He poked his head through the fence and sniffed at the present Holly had tucked under her arm. It was wrapped in shiny blue paper.

"This is for Billy, not you!" said Holly with a laugh. "Isn't he sweet? I can't wait to play with the animals."

Rose patted the little goat's fluffy head. "Do you know who else I want to see?"

"The Little Sparkles, of course!" cried Holly, bouncing up and down so that her plaits flew in the air. "I hope they're here."

The twins had met the Little Sparkles at their best friend Jenny's party. They were tiny, magical creatures who made sure parties were fun for everyone.

"As long as the Party Poopers don't come too," added Rose. "They do their best to ruin everything!"

The grubby, naughty little Party Poopers loved to spoil people's fun. At Jenny's party, they had messed up the food and got rid of the balloons. Holly and Rose had persuaded one of the Poopers to have fun instead, and he had transformed into a Little Sparkle. But there were still four Party Poopers left...

"If they do turn up, we'll be ready for them," said Holly. "Hey, look at this!"

Pinned to the trunk of a tree was a poster, which read:

Billy's
Party
This way

Underneath the writing was an arrow that pointed to one of the paths.

"Come on!" cried Holly.

The twins followed the direction of the arrow. They passed a pigsty with fat little piglets wriggling inside it, hen houses and rabbit hutches, and a sheep with newborn lambs.

NEIGGGHHH!

"Horses!" cried Rose.

They peered over a fence into a paddock with tubby ponies grazing inside it, and small wooden jumps laid out. There was even a tiny black foal. On a table were crates of apples and sacks that were marked "PONY FEED".

"Look," said Holly, "another sign."

The sign was propped against the paddock fence and it said:

The twins rushed round a bend in the path and saw Billy and his dad standing by some wooden trestle tables. Billy was wearing denim shorts, a yellow T-shirt with a bumblebee picture on the front, and a green cap. The twins ran up to him.

"Happy birthday, Billy!" called Rose. "It looks like we're the first to arrive."

"I like your buzzy bee," Holly said. She handed him his present.

"Thanks," said Billy. But he didn't smile.

"What's wrong?" cried Rose.

Billy sighed. "Something horrible has happened to my party." He pointed to the table where the food was spread out.

The twins gasped.

The jam sandwiches and sausages were speckled with green mould, the crisps and popcorn had turned to sludge, and the jelly had melted into a runny orange pool.

"You know what this means, don't you?" Holly whispered to Rose. "The Party Poopers must be here!"

2

Muddly Misery

"Everything's gone wrong," said Billy, his lip quivering. "My cake was shaped like a bumblebee, but now look at it!"

The twins stared in horror at the pile of chocolatey crumbs.

Billy's dad came over.

"Hello, girls," he sighed. "It's all very upsetting, isn't it? We were going to do face-painting, but now we can't."

The twins turned to the table with the

face-painting equipment on it. The paints had melted and run across the tabletop. The mirror was all smeary, and the stick-on whiskers were crumpled.

"Oh no!" cried Rose.

"And the balloon animals keep going wrong too," said Billy. He held up a lumpy yellow balloon animal with lots of spiky legs. "When Dad first made this one, it was a really cool giraffe. But now it looks like an ugly monster!"

"Yes, it's the strangest thing," said Billy's dad, scratching his head. "I suppose the hot weather's making everything melt and go funny."

The twins glanced at each other.

"It wasn't the heat, it was the Party Poopers," whispered Rose. "We've got to find them before they make things even worse."

The other guests started to arrive, wearing sun hats and holding presents for Billy. Jenny ran up, wearing a yellow dress and flip-flops. She hugged the twins, but her eyes widened when she saw the mess.

"Look at the sandwiches," Jenny said, "and the cake! What happened?"

"I don't know," muttered Billy. "It was going to be so fun, but..." He hung his head.

"It can still be fun," said Holly quickly. "You could go to the paddock and feed the ponies!"

"They're very cute," added Rose. "You could groom them, too."

The guests cheered. Even Billy smiled a little.

"What a good idea," said Billy's dad. "Come on, everyone."

As he led the chattering boys and

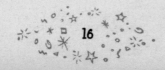

girls away towards the paddock, the
twins nipped behind a nearby chicken
house.

"We'd better stay and fix this mess,"
whispered Holly.

They waited until the other boys and

girls had gone, then came out and looked at the ruined party things.

"It's very strange that we haven't seen the Little Sparkles yet," said Rose. "I thought they would help us stop the Poopers."

'No one can stop us!" shrieked a voice.

The girls spun round. A tiny creature was hopping about on the remains of Billy's cake. He was small and round, with short arms and legs and a wonky little tail. He had grey, doughy skin, green teeth, and his face was scrunched up into a scowl.

A Party Pooper!

3

Save the Sparkles

The Party Pooper kicked crumbs in the air
and chanted:

> *"Silly Billy's party at the zoo,*
> *I'm going to poop it,*
> *whoo-hoo-hoo!"*

"No, you're not!" shouted Rose with her hands on her hips.

The Pooper glared at the twins. "You two again!" he snapped. "Well, bad luck, you dumb-dumbs. I'm turning all the fun to crumbs!" He threw a lump of icing at the twins.

"You get off poor Billy's cake!" said Holly.

"Shan't!" screeched the Pooper. He stuck out his tongue and bolted from the table.

"Quick, catch him!" cried Rose.

They charged after the Pooper. He tried to lose them, dodging behind hedges and hutches. Chickens squawked at the rustling leaves as he passed, and a sheep ran away bleating when he bounced on her woolly back.

Suddenly, the Pooper disappeared behind a rose bush. The twins dashed after him, but he was nowhere to be seen.

"We've lost him," said Rose, panting for breath.

A sweet tinkling noise, like pixie bells, drifted towards them.

"I know that sound!" said Holly, grinning. "It's the Little Sparkles!"

The twins hurried down one of the paths, following the noise. As they neared a large guinea-pig hutch, the tinkling got louder and louder.

"They must be inside here," said Rose.

Through the wire-mesh door, they could see three guinea pigs snuffling about in the hay. And floating above

them, in a haze of glitter, were the Little Sparkles. They glowed like colourful fairy lights, and were so small they could have sat in the twins' hands. Each was carrying a little party bag.

"How will we ever get out?" sighed Bubbles the pink bunny.

Peppy the tiny light-blue puppy was rattling the hutch door, trying to open it, while Princess the pony pranced up and down the hutch. Tubbs the turtle had his legs and head tucked inside his rainbow shell. In a corner was Tikki the teeny yellow kitten, singing sadly to herself.

"Don't worry," cried Holly. "We'll get you out!"

As the girls knelt down in front of the hutch door, the Little Sparkles cheered with delight and whizzed over to them, leaving behind trails of colourful glitter.

"How lovely to see you!" said Peppy,

wagging his tail.

"Why are you trapped in this hutch?" asked Rose.

"The Poopers locked us in, so we couldn't stop them pooping Billy's party," miaowed Tikki.

The Little Sparkles were invisible to everyone apart from the twins, but the guinea pigs could still hear their tinkling voices. Their ears twitched, following the sound. Just then, one of the guinea pigs seemed to notice the twins too. He stood up on his back legs and sniffed at them through the wire, his whiskers nearly knocking the Little Sparkles out of the air.

"Watch out!" cried Rose.

All the Little Sparkles dived to safety just in time. Tubbs rolled aside and Princess jumped straight over the guinea pig's head.

"It's OK, he didn't mean to," laughed Peppy, bobbing back up.

"We'd better get you out of this hutch," said Holly. "Come on, Rose!"

They both took hold of the big bolt on the door and tugged at it together. With a creak, it slid across and the door swung open.

"Hooray!" cheered Peppy as he bounded out in a shower of blue glitter. He was followed by Princess, Tikki and Bubbles,

who hopped on to Holly's shoulder.
Finally came Tubbs the turtle, who did a
head-over-heels roll out of the door, like a
clown.

"Twin-Team to the rescue again!"
Tubbs cried.

One of the guinea pigs poked his head out of the hutch too. He snuffled, his whiskers twitching.

Rose gave a shout of alarm. "Quick – he's going to escape!"

But before anybody could close the hutch door, the guinea pig leapt out and scampered away down the path.

"Oh no," cried Holly. "Now we'll have to catch him as well as stopping the Poopers!"

4

A Furry Fright

"Oh, poor guinea pig," said Bubbles, hiding behind her long ears. "He might not be safe out of his hutch!"

"Don't worry," said Rose, "we'll find him."

The twins ran down the path in the direction the guinea pig had disappeared, with the Little Sparkles floating behind them. One of the bushes they passed was shaking and a strange shrieking came from inside it.

"*Arrgghhh! Ughhhhh!*"

"What's that?" miaowed Tikki, her fur standing on end.

"Sounds like the Poopers," said Holly.

The bush's leaves rustled and there was the sound of twigs snapping.

"I think they're coming this way!" said Rose. "Let's hide and see what they're up to."

They all ducked behind another big bush. Peering out from between the branches, Holly and Rose saw four Poopers emerge. They were covered with torn-up streamers and burst balloons from Billy's party, and their eyes were wide.

"It must have been a monster," said one of them.

Another Pooper nodded, his teeth chattering with fright. "D-did you s-s-see its whiskers and its t-t-twitching nose?"

Rose glanced at Holly. "They must mean the guinea pig," she whispered.

The biggest Pooper puffed out his chest. "I wasn't scared, you sissies," he boasted to the other three Poopers. "Anyway, it's gone now. Let's go back to the party tables and start muddling again."

The four Party Poopers ran away up the path. As they went, the bits and pieces that were stuck to them fell off in grubby little piles.

The twins and the Little Sparkles came out from behind the bush. The Poopers were almost out of sight. Holly could just make out their grey, blobby little bodies.

"How can we stop them getting to the party tables before we do?" she wondered.

"I know!" yapped Peppy. "Let's use the Poopers' own mess to slow them down. Little Sparkles, get your party blowers."

In a shower of glitter, the Little

Sparkles pulled matching blowers out of their little party bags. Together they blew a tune:

Toot-toot-parp!

The twins gasped as the torn balloons

and streamers that had fallen off the Poopers lifted away from the ground. They twirled in the air, whizzing up the path. Then, with one last toot from the Little Sparkles, they landed in a heap in front of the Poopers.

The twins ran closer, careful to stay hidden behind the shrubs and plants. They held their breath as they waited to see what happened.

The first Pooper stumbled into the mess, and fell flat on the path.

SPLAT!

The next Pooper knocked into him, and then the other two.

SPLAT! SPLAT! SPLAT!

The twins cheered as the Little Sparkles flew up to join them.

"Well done, Little Sparkles!" said Holly.

The Poopers began to dust themselves off, one of them rubbing his head in confusion.

"We've slowed them down," said Rose, "but we haven't stopped them. What do we do next?"

5

Airy Monsters

Holly frowned as she thought as hard as she could. A cherry tree grew beside the path, and pinned to it was one of the signs that showed the way to Billy's birthday party. It had a bright blue arrow on it.

"I know!" she cried. "Let's move the signs. Then the Poopers will get lost..."

"...and they won't be able to find the party tables," finished Rose.

"Yes!" agreed Princess. "I can gallop quickly – I'll do it!"

The little pony flew to the cherry tree and, using her teeth, tugged the sign free. She stuck it to a tree on the other side of the path – which meant that the arrow was pointing in the opposite direction.

Then, with a swish of her glittery tail, she pranced away to move the other signs.

The Poopers were standing up now. They were still covered in dust and grumbling.

The big Pooper pointed to the sign that Princess had just moved. "This way, you twerps," he said. All the Poopers followed him, grinding their teeth.

"It worked – they're going the wrong way!" said Rose. "But how can we get them to leave the petting zoo?"

"I know!" cried Holly. "The silly Poopers thought that the guinea pig was a monster. Remember the balloon monster that Billy showed us? Maybe we can make some more and scare them away."

"Brilliant idea!" said Tubbs, roly-polying. "Yippee-doo!"

The twins raced back to the picnic area with the four remaining Little Sparkles zooming behind. On one of the tables was a pile of oddly-shaped balloons that Billy's dad had blown up earlier. Holly picked up a long, lumpy green one.

"These are perfect for making into monsters!" she said.

The twins knotted together the balloons to form strange-shaped creatures. Holly drew sharp teeth and googly eyes with felt-tips, while Rose fetched some hay from a chicken house and glued it on to give the monsters wild hairdos. The Little Sparkles blobbed jelly on the monsters' faces to make them look slimy.

"All done!" laughed Holly. She was holding a monster with five legs and a long tail. Rose's monster had an enormous red body with black spots on it. Between them, Tikki and Bubbles were holding a monster with two heads.

Princess pranced up to the tables and gasped. "Wow, those are scary!" she said. "I've moved all the signs now. The Poopers don't know where they are!"

"And I know just how we can find them before they find us," said Peppy, sniffing. "I'll follow their whiff with my nose."

He zoomed off down one of the paths, his little nose twitching and wiggling. The others followed him through some trees, past a donkey field and round a bend that led to a duck pond. A mother duck and six fluffy yellow ducklings were swimming around the lily pads.

"There they are," said Rose in a hushed voice.

The four Poopers were standing by the

pond. The big Pooper stomped his feet in the mud, sending up a gloopy spray.

"We followed the arrows, but there's no party here," he grumbled. "We need something to poop!"

The twins and the Little Sparkles crept round the edge of the pond and hid behind some tall rushes.

"OK, monsters at the ready," said
Holly. "One, two, THREE!"

They held the three balloon monsters
above the rushes.

"Raaaaaaarrr!" roared Holly.

"Grrrrrrrrrr!" growled Rose.

"Argghh!" cried the Poopers. "More monsters!"

They tried to run away, but skidded on the mud. The big Pooper fell backwards into the water.

SPLOSH!

He swam across the pond, paddling furiously and spitting out green water as he went. The mother duck quacked crossly at all the splashing. When the Pooper reached the opposite bank, he scrambled from the water and crawled underneath the nearby fence – out of the zoo.

But the other three Poopers were staring at the monsters.

'There's something funny about them," said one, crossing his arms.

"Grrrrrrrrr!" Holly shouted again.

Another Pooper nodded. "Their mouths don't move when they roar," he pointed out.

The three Poopers stomped towards the rushes.

"Quick," hissed Rose. "Make the monsters scarier!"

They roared and growled even more loudly, and waved the monsters about. But Rose's monster snagged on the sharp edge of a leaf and burst.

POP!

One of the Poopers narrowed his eyes. "They're not real monsters," he said. "They're just balloons!"

6

The Poopers are Chicken

"Oh no," whispered Holly. "What are we going to do now?"

Snatching up one of the duck feathers lying in the mud, the Pooper hopped into the rushes. He clambered up a thick stem and jabbed Holly's balloon monster with the tip of the feather.

POP!

"Take that, pretend monster!" the Pooper said with a laugh.

He then stuck the feather into the two-headed monster. But instead of just popping, the balloon came loose and whizzed through the air, making a loud raspberry noise. It looped and flew straight at the Pooper, carrying him squealing into the air and over the fence.

"Argghh!" shrieked the two remaining Poopers. They sprinted off, away from the pond.

Holly and Rose doubled over with

laughter and the air rang with the Little Sparkles' tinkling giggles.

"That got rid of him," said Holly, wiping her eyes. "The balloon monsters worked after all! Let's go and find the other two Poopers before Billy and the others get back from the ponies."

Peppy sniffed the air, catching the Poopers' whiffy scent, and led them past the baby goats in their pen, the piglets in their sty and the hutch that the guinea pig had escaped from. The trail ended at a chicken house.

The little hut was shaking on its wooden stilts, and the ladder up to the nesting boxes inside was wobbling. The

chickens were squawking and flapping their wings.

"I think I can guess why it's shaking," said Rose. The twins knelt down on a patch of grass and daisies and peered under the hut. The Little Sparkles flew low and looked under too.

Munching on the grains of spilled chicken feed was the escaped guinea pig. And behind him were two quivering little grey blobs.

"It's the Poopers!" cried Holly. "It looks like the guinea pig has cornered them for us." The Poopers were pressed up against one of the chicken house's wooden stilts. Every time the guinea pig moved, they trembled so much the whole house wobbled.

"What big chickens they are!" joked Tubbs, rolling in the air.

"Don't be scared," Rose called to the Poopers. "He won't hurt you. "

"We're NOT scared," snapped one Pooper, clinging to his friend.

"Well, come out then," said Holly.

"No, we like it under here," said the other Pooper, in a shaky voice. The guinea pig snuffled near him and he backed further into the corner.

"You know, I feel a bit sorry for them," said Rose. "We'd better get the guinea pig out from under there."

The twins plucked handfuls of daisies and grass and held them towards the guinea pig.

"Over here!" Holly called to him. "Look what we've got for you."

But the guinea pig took no notice. He carried on eating the chicken feed.

"Let me try," said Tikki. She started to sing:

"Sweet guinea-pig, dream
Of strawberries and cream,
Cucumbers and beans
And honey ice cream…"

"Argh – no!" groaned the Poopers.

"Stop that happy noise. We only like sad noises – like balloons bursting and presents breaking and..."

But Tikki kept singing.

The guinea pig's eyes drooped and he waddled dreamily out from under the chicken house.

"Well done, Tikki!" said Rose. "I'll take him to his home now." She scooped the guinea pig up into her arms like a dozy baby and carried him gently back to his hutch.

The others clapped.

As soon as Rose and the guinea pig had gone, the Poopers scrambled out too. One of them ran towards the zoo fence.

"I've had enough of monsters for one day," he said. "I'm off!" And he sprang over the fence and vanished.

The last Pooper started running towards the fence after his friend, but then he spotted Billy's picnic. He squawked with delight:

"Ha ha, you ninnies – you set me free,
Now I'll mash your delicious tea!"

He bounced towards the tables,

cackling loudly.

"Come on," shouted Holly. "After him!"

7

Tickled Pink

Holly and the Little Sparkles chased after the Pooper. He bounded on to the face-painting table and skidded on the spilled puddles of paint, mixing the colours into a muddy brown.

"Stop messing them up!" yelled Rose, racing back from the guinea pig hutches. Her shout startled the Pooper, who slipped and fell face down in the brown goo.

SQUELCH!

"Yuck!" screeched the Pooper as he stood. He was covered from head to foot with thick, brown slime.

At first he grimaced but then caught sight of himself in the mirror. "Oh, look at me," he cried. He ran closer to the mirror, sniggering. "I'm so scary," he laughed, his tubby little tummy wobbling. "I'm even scarier than that hairy monster under the chicken house." He made claws with his hands to make a scary pose. "Grrrr!"

"Hey, everyone," whispered Holly. "Remember that Pooper at Jenny's party who had so much fun..."

"...that he turned into a sweet Little Sparkle?" cried Rose.

"Maybe that's the way to make *all* Poopers change into Little Sparkles," said Holly. "We get them to have fun."

The Little Sparkles nodded.

"It's worth a try," said Peppy.

The Pooper was gnashing his teeth at the mirror. Then he clutched his sides, laughing at his own reflection.

Rose grinned and Holly stepped up to

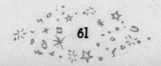

the Pooper. She gave a loud gasp and pretended to jump into the air with fright.

"Eeeek!" she squealed. "What a terrifying monster!"

Rose made her knees knock together,

as if she was so scared that she couldn't stop shaking. "Ooh, we're so frightened of you," she cried.

The Little Sparkles pretended to whimper and backed away from the Pooper.

"Help," cried Tubbs, hiding in his shell.

The Pooper hooted with laughter. He tried to snarl, but he was laughing so much he couldn't.

"Ha-ha-ha! Hee-hee-hee! HOO-HOO-HOO!"

Then, little by little, the Pooper began turning a pretty shade of pink. The more he laughed, the pinker he got. A glittering mist swirled around him.

The twins nudged each other.

"It's working!" said Rose. "He's…"

POOF!

With a shimmering burst of hundreds-and-thousands, the Pooper changed into a little pink guinea pig. He gave a delighted squeak. "I'm a Little Sparkle now!" he said.

Rose and Holly cheered and danced in a circle.

Peppy pulled out a pink balloon from his bag and the other Little Sparkles chanted:

"Spread the lovely party joy to every little girl and boy.
No more a grumpy Party Pooper, make all parties super duper."

The pink balloon blew up by itself and hung in the air. The little pink guinea pig took hold of the ribbon that was attached to it and, smiling and waving, he drifted upwards into the big blue sky.

"Goodbye!" cried Holly, waving back.

"And good luck with fixing other parties," called Rose. "We know you'll do a brilliant job."

The new Little Sparkle waved at them again as he disappeared in a haze of glitter.

"And you two did a brilliant job here," purred Tikki, rubbing against Holly's neck. "You got rid of the Poopers!"

"And just in time," woofed Peppy.

"Here comes Billy now."

They turned to see Billy, his dad and his friends in the distance, coming through the pony paddock gate.

"But the party's still in a big jumble," cried Rose. "We've got to clear up before he arrives!"

8

Little Sparkle
Razzle-Dazzle

"We'll fix it before you can say 'Happy birthday'," yapped Peppy, chasing his tail. "Just watch!"

He sat up on his back legs and held up a paw to the other Little Sparkles: "Ready ... steady ... GO!"

They zipped above the tables, sprinkling magical hundreds-and-thousands in a twinkly shower.

"Oh, wow," cried Rose. "It's so pretty!"

To the twins' amazement, the balloon animals blew themselves up, and the mirror and the tabletops became clean again. In another glittering flash, new face paints, pretty streamers and a delicious fresh picnic appeared, laid out neatly on the tables.

'There's even a new birthday cake," cried Holly. Like the cake the Poopers had ruined, it was in the shape of a bumblebee and had "Billy" piped on it. But it was much bigger, and had jelly sweets arranged around the edge to look like flowers.

"Everything's sparkling again," smiled Rose.

The magical hundreds-and-thousands faded away and the Little Sparkles swooped up into the air.

"Goodbye, Holly and Rose," they called down. "Thank you for helping us!"

"Goodbye, Little Sparkles," chorused the twins, blowing kisses.

Then, in a flash, the Little Sparkles vanished, leaving just a shimmer against the sky.

The girls turned as Billy and his guests ran up to the tables.

"We had the best time with the ponies," Billy cried, his eyes shining. "I even got to ride one!"

Then he stared at the tables.

"Wow!" he gasped. "How come everything's so nice again?"

"Who knows," said Rose. "Someone must have sorted it out."

"I'm glad they did," Billy said. "I'm starving!"

Everyone tucked into the sandwiches,

crisps and sausages. Billy's dad cut everyone a slice of the birthday cake.

"Well, I've absolutely no idea what's gone on here today," he said as he handed them out. "If I didn't know any better, I would say there was magic involved."

Holly glanced at Rose and smiled.

"Hey, Billy," called Jenny through a mouthful of sandwich. "Your party's so much fun!"

Billy grinned from ear to ear. "Yes, it is, isn't it," he said, biting into his slice of cake.

The twins looked at each other and smiled happily.

"We did it," Holly whispered to Rose.

"Yes, and I can't wait to help the Little Sparkles again," Rose said. "The Poopers are sure to try to ruin another party."

"Whatever they do, we'll beat them," said Holly. She gave Rose a high five. "Down with Poopers! Up with parties!"

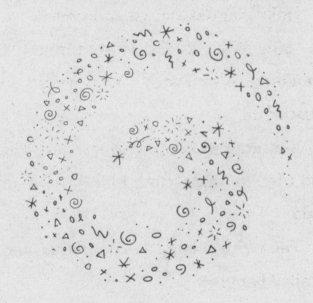

Don't miss the other

books in the series!

Little Sparkles

Party at the Pool

Have fun with these tiny magical animals!

Emily Moon

Little Sparkles

Party on the Pirate Ship

Have fun with these tiny magical animals!

Emily Moon